I0589969

First published in *Fairy Tales* 2000 by Walker Books Ltd
87 Vauxhall Walk, London SE11 5HJ

This edition published 2003

2 4 6 8 10 9 7 5 3 1

This book has been typeset in Palatino

Printed in China

British Library Cataloguing in Publication Data:
a catalogue record for this book is available from the British Library

ISBN 0-7445-9872-9

www.walkerbooks.co.uk

Beauty
and the
Beast

BERLIE DOHERTY
illustrated by JANE RAY

WALKER BOOKS
AND SUBSIDIARIES
LONDON · BOSTON · SYDNEY

There was a merchant who had three daughters and three sons. The youngest of them all was known as Beauty, and her sisters were jealous of her and treated her just as if she was their servant. They made her wash and cook while they went off to parties. But Beauty didn't mind. She was her father's favourite child; she loved him and he loved her, and that made up for everything. Many a young man came asking her to marry him, but she always said no. She loved her father too much to leave him.

One winter the merchant fell on hard times. One by one his ships were lost at sea in terrible storms, and all his wealth went with them. He had to sell their beautiful house and move into a much smaller one. The sons had to work in the fields, and the daughters to take in washing. The older girls hated this so much that they lazed in bed till ten o'clock every morning, knowing that Beauty would have got up at four to make sure the work was done. She did it willingly. It hurt her to see how distressed their father was, and she would do anything to make him happy again.

Then, one day, he received news that made him prance round the garden with joy, as if he was a young man again.

"My last ship has come home!" he sang, waving a letter at them. "We're rich again!"

He saddled his horse at once and set off to the port to sort out his business affairs. His daughters ran alongside him as far as the village well.

"Bring me lots of silk gowns!" the oldest one said.

"Bring me a little monkey!" said the middle one.

"What about you, Beauty?" The merchant laughed, full of high spirits.

"Oh," she said. "Bring me a rose, Father."

The sisters laughed at her and the merchant went on his way, singing because the morning was bright and full of promise. But by the end of the day all his happiness had vanished away. The news he had been sent was false. Far from having a ship full of merchandise, he had nothing at all. His last ship had sunk. He was completely penniless. He turned his horse for home, sad and weary though he was. It could be that he fell asleep at the reins, who knows? Anyway, he lost his way. There was a terrific snow-storm, hail came lashing down and thunder roared about him. He saw a mansion lit up in a flash of lightning and rode up towards the huge wrought-iron gates.

"Perhaps I could shelter here," he said aloud, and instantly the great gates swung open. He rode in, and the gates swung shut behind him. It was the same when he reached the mansion house. The door of the stable swung open, and he dismounted and let his horse trot in for shelter and food. He climbed the steps of the mansion and was just about to pull the bell when the great studded door swung back. He stepped inside, and it was closed behind him. There was no one to be seen, yet he had the sensation of eyes peering at him.

A bright fire sprang up in the grate; unseen hands lifted his soaked overcoat from his shoulders and his hat from his head and his gloves from his hands. He looked about him, and there was no one there.

A comfortable chair was pulled up to the fire, and he felt himself being guided towards it, and he sank down and fell asleep.

When he woke up a table had been placed at his side with tasty-smelling food steaming in a silver bowl and red wine glowing in a crystal goblet. There was still no sign of his host, but the merchant ate and drank thankfully. It was a long time since he had eaten so well. When he had finished, the table was lifted away out of sight.

The great clock chimed twelve, and one by one the candles were blown out, yet one remained, as if to light his way upstairs. The merchant stood up, yawning, and climbed the stairs. A door opened, and there was a bed freshly made, the covers turned back neatly. He knew it was meant for him, and within seconds of climbing into it he was asleep.

Next morning it was as if the storm had never been. The sun streamed through the windows. The merchant found that fine new clothes had been put out for him, and that his breakfast had been set out. He called for his host, but no one came. Yet still he had the sensation of being watched from some hidden place. He went outside to fetch his horse from the stable, and saw a garden full of sweet-smelling roses, even though it was still winter and snow laced the trees. He thought at once about Beauty, and decided to pick a rose for her before he left. He put out his hand and plucked one.

At once he heard the roar of a wild animal and dropped the rose in his terror. The bushes were clawed aside and there in front of him a hideous creature reared up on his hind legs, lashing out as if he was going to rip the merchant up into tiny shreds.

"How dare you pick my roses!" he snarled. "I have given you food and shelter willingly. How dare you steal my roses!"

The merchant flung himself on to his knees, weak with fear.

"Forgive me. Please forgive me, my lord," he begged.

"I am not 'my lord'. I am the Beast. You will die for this." The Beast dropped down on to all fours and prowled round the merchant, baring his teeth and growling.

"I beg you to let me go. I only picked

the rose for my daughter. All my sons and daughters will be watching out for me. At least let me say goodbye to them."

"Go back to your sons and daughters," the Beast roared. "But within one month you must return. Either you or one of your daughters must die. That is my bargain."

"I promise I'll come back," the merchant said, heavy with dread. Then he scrambled on to his horse and galloped home as if the wind was carrying him.

"I'm only with you for a short while," he told his sons and daughters. "I have come to say goodbye." And he told them the strange story of the mansion and the unseen servants, and the beautiful garden full of sweet roses in the snow. He gave Beauty her rose, and last of all he told them about the Beast, and of the promise he had made.

"I must go back to him," he said. "And you will never see me again, children."

"Let me go instead," Beauty said at once.

"Yes, let her go," the sisters said. "It was all her fault for asking for a rose."

At the end of the month Beauty and her father both went to the Beast's mansion. The huge gates swung open for them, and they went in slowly and full of fear. Again there was no one to be seen, and yet they both had the feeling that unseen eyes were watching them.

"Leave me now," Beauty said.

"How can I leave you here?" her father asked.

"You must," said Beauty, and sadly her father said goodbye to her and went back home.

Beauty found that wonderful things had been prepared for her: beautiful food, fine clothes, gorgeous jewels, yet she had no heart for any of them. She ate alone on her first evening, served by invisible hands. She felt eyes watching her, and knew that the Beast was with her. She could smell the stink of blood on him, and the foul reek of his breath; she could hear the scratch of his claws on the tiles, and when she turned to look at him she nearly fainted with fear.

"Do you have everything you need, Beauty?" he asked her.

"Yes, thank you," she said, wishing

with all her heart that he would go away. She couldn't bring herself to look at him again.

"I won't trouble you," he said. "But I should like to see you every day. May I come when you are dining, just to watch you eat?"

"You are the master," said Beauty. "I must do as you wish."

"No. I must do as *you* wish," said the Beast. "Will you please permit me, Beauty?"

So she said yes, and the next night when she was dining she shuddered to hear the scrape of his claws on the ground, and the rasp of his breathing behind her ear. At the end of her meal he put his paw over her trembling hand.

"Beauty, will you marry me?" he asked.

"No!" she screamed. She pushed him away and ran to her room, where she flung herself on her bed and sobbed for home. She was trapped with the Beast. It was quite clear that he had no intention of killing her, but she might as well be dead, she thought. Every night he came to her at nine, and every night he asked her to marry him, and always her answer was the same. But whenever he spoke there was such a deep sorrowing in his voice that she began to pity him.

"I am the Beast, and you are afraid of me," he said. "Forgive me."

"I'm not afraid of you now," Beauty said. "But I can't marry you."

"No," he said sadly.

"But I can be your friend," she told him. It was true. She began to look forward to his coming every evening. She was bored and lonely when he wasn't there. In a strange way that she couldn't understand, Beauty grew to like the Beast. But he was a beast. He killed the wild creatures in the woods around his mansion, and would sometimes have their blood on his paws and around his mouth when he came to see her. "Forgive me," he would say to her. "This is how I am."

One day the Beast gave her a mirror as a present, but when she looked into it she did not see her own reflection. She saw her father lying in bed in a poor room, and he looked old and sad and ill. Beauty ran to the Beast and begged him to let her go home.

"You want to leave me, Beauty?" he said, and his voice was so full of sadness that she felt tears rising in her.

"No, I don't want to leave you. Not for ever," she said. "But I want to be with my father too."

"Go to him," said the Beast. "But come back to me in a week. I can't live without you, Beauty."

So Beauty looked into the mirror again, and said "Father," and in that very instant she was back in the old house and standing at her father's bedside.

"Beauty!" he gasped. "Is it really you? I thought you were dead."

He sat up and laughed with joy. He had been wasting away with sadness, but the sight of his favourite daughter was all he needed to make him well and happy again. "Help me out of this bed," he told her. "I don't need it now."

His daughters and sons were working in the garden when they saw their father walking towards them on the arm of a beautiful stranger.

"Who's that fine lady?" the brothers marvelled.

"That's no fine lady. It's Beauty!" the oldest sister snapped.

"Just look at her, done up like a queen!" the middle sister said. "Who does she think she is!"

But Beauty was glad to give them her

jewels and her silk gown. "I don't need them," she told them. "All I need is to see my father well and happy."

"Promise me you won't ever go away again," he asked her.

"I can't promise that, Father. The Beast wants me to go back in a week."

"But you don't have to!" her oldest brother said. "We'll kill him for you."

When he said that, Beauty went pale and her eyes brimmed with tears. They all looked at her strangely.

"Why," said her father, "what's this, Beauty? I do believe you have grown fond of the Beast!"

But she turned away and couldn't speak for the odd sadness that filled her heart.

All the same, they begged her to stay with them. Her father was well and strong, but he said he would take to his bed immediately if she were to leave him again. Beauty had taken up her tasks around the house and in the fields so willingly that her sisters were determined to make her stay so they wouldn't have to work any more. On the day she was due to leave they squeezed onion juice into their eyes to make themselves cry. "Don't go! Please don't go, Beauty!" they begged her, and Beauty was moved by their tears. She felt as if her heart was being torn in two.

So she stayed, but every night she dreamed of the Beast. Nearly a week later she picked up her mirror, and instead of her reflection she saw him. His eyes were closed, and he was slumped on the ground, too weak to move. She gave a cry of horror. "Beast!" she sobbed. "Don't die! Oh please don't die!" and instantly she was running through the great wrought-iron gates of the mansion, running through the gardens, running through the sweet-smelling rose bower and into the wild part where the Beast liked to hunt.

"Beast!" she called. "Where are you? Oh, where are you, Beast?"

At last she saw him stretched out in the long grass. His eyes were closed, and he was as still as death. She ran to him and cradled his head in her arms. "Don't die. Please don't die!" she sobbed. "I love you, Beast."